At the Art Mart

Story by Suzanne Barchers
Illustrated by George Ulrich
Designed by Six Red Marbles

 "Let's go to the art mart," says Clark. "We will find Barbara a perfect birthday present there!"

Mark and Clark
wave goodbye to
Mom, Dad, Nancy,
and Barbara.

 Mark and Clark get
on the bus. They
ride the bus to the
art mart at the park.

"Clark, look at all the carts," says Mark. "Let's start looking!"

Mark and Clark
start at the
bark cart.

"A bone is fun for a dog in the sun," says Clark. "But it's not for Barbara. Let's go on."

 Mark and Clark run to the yarn cart.

Mark looks at Clark and says, "This is fine yarn for a cat in a barn, but it's not for Barbara."

Mark and Clark zip to the music cart.

Clark picks up a
harp and says,
"A harp is fun to
play in the park.
But a harp is too
hard for Barbara."

Mark and Clark
dash to the
charm cart.

"We cannot miss
with a charm for
big sis," says Mark.
"But it's not for
Barbara."

 Mark and Clark rush to the scarf cart.

"A scarf may be a good bet for Mom, but it's not for Barbara," says Clark.

◉ Mark and Clark jog to the car cart.

"We can go far
with this kind of
car," says Clark.
"But it's not for
Barbara."

 Mark and Clark stare at the tart cart.

"Let's share a tart," says Clark. "We'll both eat part. And we can think about what to get Barbara."

 Mark and Clark skip to the jar cart.

"Grandma likes
jars for her candy
bars," says Mark.
"But they are not
for Barbara."

 Mark and Clark
march to the
yard-art cart.
"This is a cool cart,"
says Clark.

"Dad might like this yard art," says Clark. "But it's not for Barbara."

 Mark and Clark
go to the card cart.
Mark picks up
a card.

He says, "Let's get this card. It's not a gift, but it is a start. Will we ever find anything for Barbara?"

 "So far we have seen bones and yarn, harps and charms. We've seen scarves and cars, tarts and jars."

"We've seen art for the yard. We got a fine card. But what about a gift for Barbara?"

 "It's getting late, Mark. Soon the park will get dark."

"We've looked near
and far. We need
to rush, Clark."

🔖 Mark and Clark
dart to the
craft cart.

"This is it!" says Mark. "We know what to get for the best gift yet!"

 "With paints from this cart, Barbara can make her own art," says Mark. "This is for Barbara!"

harp

flute

bars

spoke

truck

car

tart cart

jar cart

dog

Mom

yard-art cart

big sis

cat

craft cart

Words You're Learning
R-Controlled Vowels

Skill Words

art	carts	harp	part
bark	charm	harps	scarf
barn	charms	jar	start
bars	Clark	jars	tart
car	dark	march	tarts
card	dart	Mark	yard
cars	far	mart	yarn
cart	hard	park	

Sight Words

about	all

Challenging Words

anything	from	might	share
Barbara	getting	music	so
birthday	good	Nancy	soon
candy	goodbye	near	stare
cool	Grandma	own	there
craft	kind	play	we'll
eat	looked	present	we've
find	looking	scarves	